*To Max and Matilda, a hop, skip
and a jump along the way.*
R.A.

*For Baby Betty. I hope you enjoy reading
this book as much as you will nibbling it! x*
N.D.

WALKER BOOKS
AND SUBSIDIARIES
LONDON · BOSTON · SYDNEY · AUCKLAND

First published 2017 by Walker Books Ltd, 87 Vauxhall Walk, London SE11 5HJ • Text © 2017 Ronda Armitage • Illustrations © 2017 Nikki Dyson • The right of Ronda Armitage and Nikki Dyson to be identified as author and illustrator respectively of this work has been asserted by them in accordance with the Copyright, Designs and Patents Act 1988 • This book has been typeset in Archer • Printed in China
• British Library Cataloguing in Publication Data: a catalogue record for this book is available from the British Library
ISBN 978-1-4063-6155-1 (hb) • ISBN 978-1-4063-7798-9 (pb) • www.walker.co.uk • 10 9 8 7 6 5 4 3 2 1

A MIGHTY BITEY CREATURE

Ronda Armitage

ILLUSTRATED BY Nikki Dyson

All was quiet
in the jungle, until...

"OU-OU-OUCH!" cried Frog.

"WHO DID THAT?
Who bit my lovely green bottom?
Something MIGHTY and
super-sharp BITEY!
I must tell Lion about
this nasty creature.
He's King of the Jungle,
he'll know what to do."

FWISHY-WISHY
FWISHY-WISHY

"Something's coming, something's after me ...

I'm scared!" Frog said.

"Hello, Frog," said Monkey.
"Where are you going in such a hurry?"

"Sh-sh-shh!" whispered Frog.
"Something's coming ...
something MIGHTY and
super-sharp BITEY.
It bit my bottom so it might bite YOU.
I'm off to tell King Lion.
He'll know what to do."

"EE-EE-EEEK!"

shrieked Monkey.
"WHAT WAS THAT?
Something's bitten my hairy bottom, too.
It's something MIGHTY
and super-sharp BITEY.
Oh please, dear Frog.
Can I come with you?"

snuffly-shuffly
snuffly

"Something's after us! It might EAT us!

I'm scared!" Monkey said.

"Hello, you two!" said Zebra.
"Where are you rushing off to?"

"Sh-sh-shh!
There's a snuffly-shuffly
creature coming," croaked Frog.

"A creature that's MIGHTY
and super-sharp BITEY,"
whispered Monkey.
"It bit our bottoms and it might bite YOU.
We must tell King Lion.
He'll know what to do."

"YA-A-A-HOO!"

shrieked Zebra.
"WHAT WAS THAT?
Something bit my stripy bottom.
Please wait, you two.
I'd like to come with you."

"I'm SCARED!" Zebra said.

"Guard your bottoms and run, run, run, as fast as you can!"

BANG!

"You noisy creatures," growled King Lion.
"You've woken me from my nap."

"Oh, please, great King," said Frog.
"We need your help. Out there is a massive,
 MIGHTY BITEY creature with super-duper,
 ship-shape-sharp teeth."

"It bit my beautiful bottom," said Zebra.

"It's coming after us!" wailed Frog.

"I have the ideal solution," said Lion.
"I'm BIG and BRAVE and HUNGRY.
 I'll hunt this MIGHTY creature
 and I'll gobble it up for dinner."

"GR-RR-RR-AHH!" roared Lion.
"WHAT WAS THAT?
Something has bitten my very royal bottom.
Something MASSIVELY MIGHTY with
super-duper, ship-shape-sharp BITEY teeth.
Where is it? Where's the dangerous creature?"

Fwishy-Wishy Fwishy-Wishy

"It's over there," whispered Monkey.

Snuffly-Shuffly snuffly-Shuffly

"It's coming closer," shrieked Frog.

"STAND BACK!" commanded Lion.

"Oh," said Frog.
"What sort of creature is that?"

"I don't know," said Zebra.
"What a teeny weeny thing."

"Teeny weeny with big oogly eyes,"
  said Monkey.

"This teeny weeny, oogly-eyed creature
  is a baby," announced Lion.
"A bush baby."

"Ah-ha," said Lion, puffing out his chest.
"Now I know why that bush baby bit us."

"Clever Lion," said Monkey.

"King of the Jungle," said Frog.

"The poor little creature is hungry," said Lion.
"And so am I."

"Will you gobble it up for dinner?" asked Frog.

"Certainly not," said Lion. "I don't eat babies."

At dinner time, Monkey ate bananas, Zebra munched grass, Frog caught some mosquitoes and Lion chewed on a large, juicy mango.

And that mighty bitey baby had a little nibble of this,
a tiny bit of that and a large chew of Lion's mango.

And later, Lion made a tiny bed for
the baby, before he sang it to sleep.
"Good night, baby. Sleep tight, baby.
And don't let your teeth bite ...
ANY MORE BOTTOMS."